One Hundred Aphorisms of Life

Samuel Onyeche

Ukiyoto Publishing

All global publishing rights are held by

Ukiyoto Publishing

Published in 2023

Content Copyright © Samuel Onyeche

ISBN 9789359208053

All rights reserved.
No part of this publication may be reproduced, transmitted, or stored in a retrieval system, in any form by any means, electronic, mechanical, photocopying, recording or otherwise, without the prior permission of the publisher.

The moral rights of the author have been asserted.

This is a work of fiction. Names, characters, businesses, places, events, locales, and incidents are either the products of the author's imagination or used in a fictitious manner. Any resemblance to actual persons, living or dead, or actual events is purely coincidental.

This book is sold subject to the condition that it shall not by way of trade or otherwise, be lent, resold, hired out or otherwise circulated, without the publisher's prior consent, in any form of binding or cover other than that in which it is published.

I dedicate this book

to

Humanity

Acknowledgements

The wisdom that births knowledge, the muse that births creativity, and the thought that births tangible things are but gifts from the Almighty God. I return all the Glory to him; whose healing leaves no scar. With a face of a thousand joy, I say thank you to my lovely parents; Mr. and Mrs. Jonathan Onyeche, and to my ever-caring sister; Joy Chidinma Tochuwkwu. May the Good Lord greatly reward them for their incessant support, love, and encouragement.

As the wings of the great eagle are made up of different strands of individual feathers, so is my writing journey, and as such; I am very grateful to Prof. Kontein Trinya, Prof. Samuel Otamiri, Prof. Samuel Amaele, Prof. Ibiere Ken-maduako, Dr. Jawaz Jaffri. Dr. Anthony Orlu, Dr. Wellington Nwogu, Dr. Uzo Nwamara, Dr. Ibiwari Ikiriko, Poet Saro Ogumba, Uncle Philip Amadi and Mr. Promise C J, I am forever indebted to them.

I passionately, press the trigger of a thousand gunshots of gratitude, as I say thank you to poet John Chinaka Onyeche, Engr. Abinye D. C. Nwankwo, Aunty Boma Samuel, Nket Godwin, Mr. Jacob Irikana, and my lovely friend; Miss Goodness Obinnah. My success story can not be told without their names being mentioned. I am so blessed to have these amazing people in my life.

Synopsis

One Hundred Aphorisms is a brilliant book endowed with metaphysical, philosophical, and proverbial aesthetics. Embellished with instructive, motivational, and didactic theories of life that are medicinal to the mind and uplifting to the soul. The aphorisms are meticulously crafted with simple and enthralling diction, woven to motivate, educate and inspire.

It is an embodiment of divine wisdom, wit, knowledge, and experiences that life has painfully taught the writer; no wonder he says "Experience is not plucked from the tree or dropped from the sky. The pain that couldn't kill you, the river that couldn't drown you, and the destructions that couldn't mar you, build a reservoir of experiences within you". In the pages of this book, you will find transformation, joy, courage, ideas, and the essence of your existence.

Samuel Alozie Onyeche
The Poetic Preacher
Port Harcourt, Nigeria 2023

* Foreword *

Whether written or spoken, words are eternal. They outlive their speakers or writers. They do not rust or rot; they are evergreen and powerful; they are stronger than weapons of war. We create with words. We destroy with words. History is replete with classic examples where words and walls have been created and destroyed such as the fallen walls of Jericho and the amalgamation of Nigeria. Words can be as powerful as machinery if humans master the art of using them in peculiar situations where they become applicable substitutes or the only available means of achieving a feat. They are indubitably therapeutic, too; instructive, informative, and educative. They have the force that elongates and/or shortens life, too. Therefore, the significance of words cannot be overstated.

Samuel Onyeche, mostly known as a poet with this treatise, has henceforth, registered himself as a writer of proverbial and philosophical aesthetics; a collection of wise words created from his African oral tradition.

However, aphorisms are synonymous with proverbs. Pertinently, Chinua Achebe posits that "proverbs are the palm oil with which words are eaten." Achebe's assertion indicates that proverbs are lubricants that soften the skin of words, thereby making them look incredibly appealing.

The young philosopher in Aphorism Six writes: "Be humble and kind for your beauty and my elegant visage are but food for ants and maggots." This underlines the transient nature of mankind. Since man dies and becomes food for ants and maggots; it, therefore, becomes imperative that man lives a life of humbleness and kindness, if his soul must find rest afterwards.

Aphorism Thirteen, thus: "The journey to greatness is like the native way of hunting for honey; smokes, scorches, and stings are not left out," reveals that a prize can only be won by someone willing to pay the price; hence, no cross, no crown! It goes further to mean that no one wins a war that he/she did not fight. Conversely, bees are the storehouses of honey which means that the hunter cannot access honey without conquering the bee. Thus, he inescapably passes through some painful processes before getting hold of the honey.

The writer in Aphorism Thirty, thus states: "He who chose to be a farmer of flowers should not forget that flowers do not bear fruits; they blossom." This maxim draws attention to some businesses, adventures, or ventures that are futile, which do not merit the attention of whoever expects fruits from his/her labors. In Aphorism Fifty-four, "Bathe your mind in the river of books and nourish your brain with the mystery of words" reveals the undeniable impact of reading to hone skills set and competencies as well as oil that prevents it from decay. The saying furthermore unearths the profound nature of words.

It is noteworthy that the writer's wealth of philosophy, perception, and wisdom is enormous, rare, and a thousand times ahead of his age.

Onyeche's _One Hundred Aphorisms of Life_ is a collected assortment of shrewd dictums of life and knowledge, warily written in simple but deep language for the understanding of readers at all levels. It is an insightful version of the written word. I recommend the book to all literate people around the world.

- *Wellington Nwogu, Ph.D.,*

Poet Laureate and author of _Well of Wisdom._

Contents

Aphorism One — 2
Aphorism Two — 3
Aphorism Three — 4
Aphorism Four — 5
Aphorism Five — 6
Aphorism Six — 7
Aphorism Seven — 8
Aphorism Eight — 9
Aphorism Nine — 10
Aphorism Ten — 11
Aphorism Eleven — 12
Aphorism Twelve — 13
Aphorism Thirteen — 14
Aphorism Fourteen — 15
Aphorism Fifteen — 16
Aphorism Sixteen — 17
Aphorism Seventeen — 18
Aphorism Eighteen — 19
Aphorism Nineteen — 20
Aphorism Twenty — 21
Aphorism Twenty One — 22
Aphorism Twenty Two — 23
Aphorism Twenty Three — 24
Aphorism Twenty Four — 25

Aphorism Twenty Five	26
Aphorism Twenty Six	27
Aphorism Twenty Seven	28
Aphorism Twenty Eight	29
Aphorism Twenty Nine	30
Aphorism Thirty	31
Aphorism Thirty One	32
Aphorism Thirty Two	33
Aphorism Thirty Three	34
Aphorism Thirty Four	35
Aphorism Thirty Five	36
Aphorism Thirty Six	37
Aphorism Thirty Seven	38
Aphorism Thirty Eight	39
Aphorism Thirty Nine	40
Aphorism Forty	41
Aphorism Forty One	42
Aphorism Forty Two	43
Aphorism Forty Three	44
Aphorism Forty Four	45
Aphorism Four Five	46
Aphorism Forty Six	47
Aphorism Forty Seven	48
Aphorism Forty Eight	49
Aphorism Forty Nine	50
Aphorism Fifty	51

Aphorism Fifty One	52
Aphorism Fifty Two	53
Aphorism Fifty Three	54
Aphorism Forty Four	55
Aphorism Fifty Five	56
Aphorism Fifty Six	57
Aphorism Fifty Seven	58
Aphorism Fifty Eight	59
Aphorism Fifty Nine	60
Aphorism Sixty	61
Aphorism Sixty One	62
Aphorism Sixty Two	63
Aphorism Sixty Three	64
Aphorism Sixty Four	65
Aphorism Sixty Five	66
Aphorism Sixty Six	67
Aphorism Sixty Seven	68
Aphorism Sixty Eight	69
Aphorism Sixty Nine	70
Aphorism Seventy	71
Aphorism Seventy One	72
Aphorism Seventy Two	73
Aphorism Seventy Three	74
Aphorism Seventy Four	75
Aphorism Seventy Five	76
Aphorism Seventy Six	77

Aphorism Seventy Seven	78
Aphorism Seventy Eight	79
Aphorism Seventy Nine	80
Aphorism Eighty	81
Aphorism Eighty One	82
Aphorism Eighty Two	83
Aphorism Eighty Three	84
Aphorism Eighty Four	85
Aphorism Eighty FIve	86
Aphorism Eighty Six	87
Aphorism Eighty Seven	88
Aphorism Eighty Eight	89
Aphorism Eighty Nine	90
Aphorism Ninety	91
Aphorism Ninety One	92
Aphorism Ninety Two	93
Aphorism Ninety Three	94
Aphorism Ninety Four	95
Aphorism Ninety Five	96
Aphorism Ninety Six	97
Aphorism Ninety Seven	98
Aphorism Ninety Eight	99
Aphorism Ninety Nine	100
Aphorism One Hundred	101
About the Author	*102*

Aphorisms of Life

Are you ready for a life transforming experience, If yes, then meditatively read the Aphorisms one after the other and follow its principles. For Life is a forest of thorns and we are like snails, everyone heaves his shell.

Aphorism One

Life is a beautiful war, if you can't find the soil. Grow on stones.

(Photo credit to the owner)

Aphorism Two

Experience is not plucked from the tree or dropped from the sky. The pain that couldn't kill you, the river that couldn't drown you, and the destructions that couldn't mar you build a reservoir of experiences within you.

Aphorism Three

When you walk through the forest of pain, stomp at every intersection. Because your tears will surely dry up, but the footprints will become statues of strength and encouragement for those who take notice.

Aphorism Four

Do not be ashamed to hold onto what's broken, hoping for wholeness. For even the greatest of men once stood in ruined days.

Aphorism Five

We become slaves of knowledge and masters of Ignorance, when we know all books but do not know love; the metaphor for God.

Aphorism Six

Be humble and kind for your beauty and my elegant visage are but food for ants and maggots.

Aphorism Seven

If you sleep, when you ought to run,
You will certainly run, when it's time to sleep

Aphorism Eight

There is no magic in success, for even a miracle has its price.

Aphorism Nine

The son who sits and eats with his father
Grows with the eye and mind of elders

Aphorism Ten

Parents are the first book their children read.

Aphorism Eleven

If you ignore the Mirror
You become a public Mirror

Aphorism Twelve

Those who do not bear the dream will show you trillions of impossibilities and give you beautiful reasons why you should kill the dream.

Aphorism Thirteen

The journey to greatness is like the native way of hunting for honey, smokes, scorch, and stings are not left out.

Aphorism Fourteen

Be careful of what you admire, lest you admire the beauty and melody of a ticking bomb.

Aphorism Fifteen

It is unwise to desire the beauty of a butterfly and loathe the trivialities and the visage of a caterpillar. Gold doesn't grow on trees.

Aphorism Sixteen

Lying doesn't just make people scrutinize your words. It also gives indelible scars to your truth(s).

Aphorism Seventeen

Words are windows of the heart
But not windows to the mind.

Aphorism Eighteen

There is wisdom in not being too quick to speak.

Aphorism Nineteen

It's okay to make mistakes,
but don't let trust die in your hands.

Aphorism Twenty

There are three things a house should not lack: a **Mirror,** a **Book,** and a **Pen**.

Aphorism Twenty One

Perseverance and hard work
are the fire that refine men as gold

Aphorism Twenty Two

A house built of gold does not fear flames.

Aphorism Twenty Three

The greatest need of a man is Peace of Mind.

Aphorism **Twenty Four**

The art of positive thinking is the womb that gives birth to the Impossible

Aphorism Twenty Five

Heroes are men who chose courage over fear.

But the shadow of a coward could make him jump fence.

Aphorism **Twenty Six**

We become slaves to our conscience and cowards to justice when we tell lies that murder Justice.

Aphorism Twenty Seven

Greatness begins with humble decisions that turn persistent efforts into tangible desires, desires that kings admire.

Aphorism Twenty Eight

As poverty is the true test of patience,
That's how wealth is the true test of pride.

Aphorism **Twenty Nine**

Until you stand in front of mirrors and open yourself like a book, you will never see the height of your hubris.

Aphorism Thirty

He who chose to be a farmer of flowers

should not forget, that flowers do not bear fruits; they blossom.

Aphorism **Thirty One**

Insanity begins not only with wry laughter but also with unspeakable mysteries.

Aphorism **Thirty Two**

There are various types of thunder,
I dread the one in the human tongue.

Aphorism **Thirty Three**

A sound mind and a healthy body
are the greatest assets one can have.

Aphorism **Thirty Four**

The mind is an egg, fertilize it.

Aphorism Thirty Five

True change begins in the mind for thoughts are what men become.

Aphorism **Thirty Six**

When a wise man begets a foolish son,
he questions his pintle, he dies while alive.

Aphorism Thirty Seven

There are different shades of wisdom, but the wisest; is knowing when to speak and when to be silent.

Aphorism Thirty Eight

Ignorance is like pregnancy
you can't hide it for too long.

Aphorism **Thirty Nine**

If you refuse to build yourself, you will become an uncompleted building.(A home for hoodlums)

Aphorism Forty

Dream and Destiny
may begin with the same letter
but are two roads to different fates.

Aphorism **Forty One**

Humble yourself and spit on no man.
For the night cloud, owns the moon
and the stars.

Aphorism **Forty Two**

You will become more beautiful if you break your ego and allow people who can see your errors, be your mirror.

Aphorism **Forty Three**

A cord broken three times
bears three knots.

Aphorism **Forty Four**

Calculation aren't just a stuff in mathematics
It is the tool for survival.

Aphorism **Four Five**

School is neither the classroom nor the geographical location of teaching and learning processes. School lives in the pages of powerful books, and in the mouth of learned men.

Aphorism **Forty Six**

There are various types of libraries. Prof. Ozo-mekuri Ndimele, Prof. Kontein Trinya, Prof. Samuel Amaele, and Prof. Samuel Otamiri, these men are mobile libraries.

Aphorism **Forty Seven**

Golds do bath in a pool of water
They bath in the furnace of fire.

Aphorism **Forty Eight**

Writing is one of the ways poets breathe

Aphorism **Forty Nine**

Reading unlocks not only doors of the eyes but doors of the mind.

Aphorism **Fifty**

Books are not just the product of a sound mind,
They are the technologies of healthy brains.

Aphorism **Fifty One**

Beauty is a weapon that wise men fear
and wisdom is a gift that frightens even kings.

Aphorism Fifty Two

Good books are the ornaments of the mind,
and shouldn't just be element for shelf decorations.

Aphorism Fifty Three

Good Poetry is medicine for the soul

Aphorism **Forty Four**

Bathe your mind in the river of books and nourish your brain with the mystery of words.

Aphorism **Fifty Five**

Life they say " is no bed of roses" , But a smart and hard working person, can make life a bed of hisbicus or even Jesmines.

Aphorism **Fifty Six**

Books are not just the product of a sound mind
They are the technologies of healthy brains.

Aphorism **Fifty Seven**

When your love for money supersedes your love for humanity, inhumanity becomes inevitable.

Aphorism **Fifty Eight**

The devil's gift is but beautiful bait.

Aphorism **Fifty Nine**

When you read books with passion and thirst for knowledge. You aren't just reading, you're communicating with the spirit of the author.

Aphorism Sixty

We are sculptures of beautiful ice,
Melt we must, as days go by.

Aphorism Sixty One

Three scars are enough to destroy a god,
Beware of scars that kill destiny.

Aphorism Sixty Two

Scars are not the footprints of dead wounds.
They are the indelible tears on the skin of memory

Aphorism Sixty Three

It's okay to be angry but uncontrolled anger is a time bomb.

Aphorism Sixty Four

A thoughtful mind is a great asset
We become the content of our thought.

Aphorism Sixty Five

True respect doesn't exist alone
It's accompanied by fragile fear and trembling.

Aphorism Sixty Six

Only cowards loathe truth and enjoy the temporary solace of fibs that soon grow into thorns and spikes

Aphorism Sixty Seven

Sages build walls, geniuses build men

Aphorism Sixty Eight

The shrub that wants to be a tall tree
Should also be prepared to wrestle with the wind.

Aphorism Sixty Nine

The sick-bed and the death mat know
that life is a beautiful vanity.

Aphorism Seventy

What you seek is in the palm of your hands
 Don't be too blind to see.

Aphorism **Seventy One**

Those who break hearts
do not know, they are breaking their names too.

Aphorism Seventy Two

Arrogance and insanity share a common boundary, as the madman is ignorant of his illness, so is the arrogant, ignorant of their deadly disease.

Aphorism Seventy Three

You may not know, how far your little efforts can go—Take a step now. Because not trying is the worst mistake in life

Aphorism **Seventy Four**

A river that embraces its source, runs not dry.

Aphorism Seventy Five

Cooking is a survival skill and shouldn't be gender-based. But a lady who can't cook good food is worse than an English graduate who can't define Noun.

Aphorism Seventy Six

Thinking is free, but refined thoughts are expensive;
For the refinery of thoughts is full of gold and thorns.

Aphorism Seventy Seven

Greed begins when less wants more
And more craves for more.

Aphorism Seventy Eight

The mirror knows you better
than you know yourself— be her friend.

Aphorism Seventy Nine

Geniuses do not fall from the sky. Perseverance, repetition, and continuous practice build ordinary men into geniuses.

Aphorism **Eighty**

In vain do baskets learn the art of holding water, they still can't be used in place of waterpots.

Aphorism **Eighty One**

When you are given a trumpet, do not be in a hurry to blow your tune. Play the donor's favorite songs first.

Aphorism **Eighty Two**

Earth is a paradox &
We are but lustrous letters
written on weary waters.

Aphorism **Eighty Three**

Those who have tombstones in every corner of their home. do not pin their hopes on things that breathe.

Aphorism **Eighty Four**

There's nothing wrong with wanting to dig up your dead (your loved one), but what's there to find?

Aphorism **Eighty FIve**

The grave will spit on your bones
If you die with your dreams.

Aphorism **Eighty Six**

Death is the mystery storm
that puts out candles of a beautiful dream.

Aphorism **Eighty Seven**

Floods may wash away our footprint from the sands of time, but neither floods nor thousands of rain can wash away the footprints of good deeds filed and in the hearts of grateful men.

Aphorism **Eighty Eight**

Lust may wear the skin of love
But time and troubles unveil all mask

Aphorism **Eighty Nine**

Ignorance is a brickless prison
With fear as the jailer man.

Aphorism Ninety

Apologies do not heal broken hearts
    It only patches pain.

Aphorism Ninety One

Every great man is a basket of tales.
For life is a skillful weaver.

Aphorism **Ninety Two**

Don't just do what only makes you happy
do what gives you inner peace

Aphorism **Ninety Three**

It is one thing to find a flower
Another— to hold and cherish thorns.

Aphorism **Ninety Four**

The load may be heavy, oppressing your neck
But don't look at the weight, look at the value.

Aphorism **Ninety Five**

Love is the miracle in your heart
Yet you climb mountains in search of it.

Aphorism Ninety Six

To love is to learn, to learn the act of forgiveness, and marriage is to learn; how to turn offenses into laughter

Aphorism **Ninety Seven**

A kiss is not just the handshake of four lips.
It is the transaction of life or venom.

Aphorism **Ninety Eight**

Don't call it love until it is tried by fire and time.

Aphorism **Ninety Nine**

Don't be too busy to be loved
And don't be too available to be hated

Aphorism **One Hundred**

Hearing from God Almighty is the greatest gift a human being can have.

About the Author

SAMUEL ONYECHE

(Poet, Literary Critic & Philosopher)

SAMUEL ONYECHE is a passionate teacher, a gifted writer, and a performance poet, He is from the Niger Delta region of Nigeria and was born on the 16th of March 1989 in Etche local government area, Rivers State.

Onyeche has received several awards and honors locally and Internationally, he has also featured in many international anthologies namely: Tamikio L. Dooley's *Pens of Artists 2022 United States of America, Poets for Peace Poetry Anthology Tunisia 2022, Coach Behar Indian Anthology 2022.* And has the following books to his name: *Ijikrika; Canticles From Africa, On the Wings of a Butterfly, A Casserole of Kisses (co-authored), Parasites in*

*Paradise, Echoes of Kettledrums(co-authored), The Letter; An Epistolary Poetry, The Muse of Love, (**Co-authored**) **Song of my Country*** and many other works of literature. He holds a Bachelor of Education Degree (B.ED) in English and Literary Studies and a Master of Arts Degree (M.A) in literature from the Ignatius Ajuru University of Education Port Harcourt, Nigeria. Call or Whatsapp Samuel on +2348131181492.

www.ingramcontent.com/pod-product-compliance
Lightning Source LLC
LaVergne TN
LVHW041613070526
838199LV00052B/3123